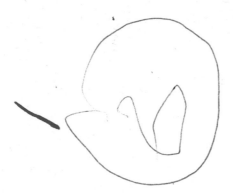

GRANDMA IS SOMEBODY SPECIAL

Story and Pictures by Susan Goldman

ALBERT WHITMAN & Company, Chicago

To Hu,
Katie, John
and Peter

Library of Congress Cataloging in Publication Data

Goldman, Susan.
    Grandma is somebody special.
    (A self-starter book)
    SUMMARY: A young child enjoys visiting her
grandmother in a tall apartment building in a big city.
    1. Grandmothers—Fiction.   I. Title.
PZ7.G5693Gr   [E]   76-18980
ISBN 0-8075-3034-4

When I go to Grandma's, we make up the cot—

—and push it close to Grandma's big bed.

At home, Mommy lets me have my own room.

But Grandma lets me share hers.

2

I look around to see if everything's the same.

"Who's that baby in the picture?" I ask.
(I always ask that.)
"That's your mommy when she was little,"
says Grandma.
"Let's look at more pictures," I say.

5

Grandma gets the albums.
I turn the pages while
Grandma tells me who is who.

"What's that noise outside?" I ask.

"Fire engines," says Grandma.

7

We go out on the balcony to look.
Mommy likes birds and trees, but
Grandma and I like fire engines and buses.

I ask, "Can we ride on the bus sometime?"
"Maybe tomorrow," says Grandma.
"Can I see where you work?"
"Yes," says Grandma. "And I'll show you
where I go to school."

9

Mommy stays home with the baby and me.
But Grandma goes out to her office,
and to school, too.

The sun goes down behind the tall buildings,
and suddenly it's cold.

I'm glad I forgot to bring my sweater
because Grandma lets me wear her blue one.
We push up the sleeves to make it fit.

It's soft, like Grandma, I think.

"I'm hungry," I say next.

"Then let's fix dinner," says Grandma.

13.

Mommy cooks Daddy's favorites, but Grandma cooks mine. Stuffed cabbage with soup, mashed potatoes, carrots, and fancy cookies from the bakery for dessert.

14

Grandma gives me tastes
with the big cooking spoon
and lets me stir.

15

When everything is ready, we sit down.
Mommy makes me sip my soup,
but Grandma lets me slurp it.
She shows me how to blow the soup
to make it cool.

16

When I'm done, I run to the closet
where Grandma keeps the toys.
There's a pegboard, crayons and paper.

17

I draw a picture for Grandma
and show it to her.

She hangs it right up on the kitchen door.

19

"Now let's play cards," I say.
"Okay," says Grandma.
She doesn't mind losing.

Then we read all the books I've brought.
Sometimes Mommy is too busy to read to me,
but Grandma isn't. She listens to everything
I say about the stories. And then we just talk.

"How about a bath?" asks Grandma.
I pour the bubble bath into
Grandma's pink tub.

Mommy says I'm big enough
to bathe myself,
but Grandma likes to help me.

22

When I'm done, she wraps me
in a towel, holds me on her lap,
and sings the songs she used
to sing to Mommy.

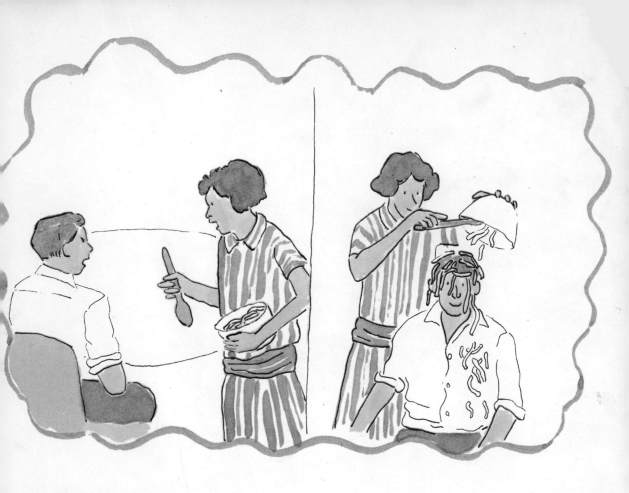

Then she tells my favorite story.
It's about the time she had a fight
with Grandpa and dumped a bowl
of noodles on his head.

I put on my pajamas,
and Grandma brushes my hair
with her big silver brush.
Mommy says I'm big enough
to brush my own hair, but
Grandma likes to do it for me.

26

I look through Grandma's jewelry box.
There are the ring and locket that
Grandpa gave her. And the amber beads
she bought with her first paycheck.
She says she will give them to me
when I grow up.

27

I get under the covers, and Grandma
tucks me in.

I hug her tight, the way I hug Mommy.
They both say the same thing—
"Good night, sleep tight. See you in
the morning light."

"Grandma," I ask, "did you say that
to Mommy when she was little?"
"Yes," says Grandma.

"I thought so!"
That's how Mommy learned it!

29

I wish I were at Grandma's now!